If Grandma Were Here

A Book of Memories

by Amber L. Bradbury

Illustrated by Jessica Corbett

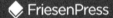 FriesenPress

Suite 300 - 990 Fort St
Victoria, BC, V8V 3K2
Canada

www.friesenpress.com

ISBN
978-1-5255-7248-7 (Hardcover)
978-1-5255-7249-4 (Paperback)
978-1-5255-7250-0 (eBook)

1. JUVENILE FICTION, FAMILY, MULTIGENERATIONAL

Distributed to the trade by The Ingram Book Company

This book is dedicated
to my great-grandmothers,
Regina Morgan and Martha Parker,
my grandmothers, Priscilla Hogan and Viola
Mitchell, and lastly, my mother, Yvonne Hogan.
Growing up, I had the honor of having these strong yet
compassionate women in my life. I was able to learn many
significant life lessons that I will always hold close to my
heart. Although they are no longer here, each day they are in my
thoughts. I often find myself imagining things we would be doing
together if they were here.

I'd also like to dedicate this book to my children, Jayden, Giselle,
and Savannah, who keep my imagination flowing. My hope is that
whenever they open a page of this book, they remember how
much they are loved. To my father, John, who never gave up on
me and always believed in me—even when I didn't believe in
myself. Lastly, to my husband, Nate, who is one of the most
hardworking, loyal, and loving people I know. Thank you for
giving that extra push I needed to get this book done. I am
forever grateful.

Lastly, I'd like to dedicate this book to all
mothers. May this book serve as a pathway
to your endearing legacy.

If Grandma were here,

she would give you
a big hug and kiss.
She would pinch your
chubby cheeks.

If Grandma were here,

you would hop in her
pearly white Cadillac.
Then hit the road to an
adventure far away!

If Grandma were here,

she would take you to the museum. You would see your favorite dinosaur and a T-Rex!

Roar!

If Grandma were here,

you'd go to the beach and build
a GIANT sandcastle.
She'd watch you splash in the
waves and play in the warm
summer sun.

If Grandma were here,

she would take you to
dance lessons.
She'd watch through
the window as you do your
best moves.

If Grandma were here,

she would give you a small shovel
and gloves. You would help her plant
colorful flowers in the butterfly
garden. Keep an eye out for Monarch
butterflies flying by!

If Grandma were here,

she'd tell you to pick out

a game to play. Stack the blocks so high.

Carefully take out each block.

But don't knock the tower over!

Let's see who wins!

If Grandma were here,

you'd put on your special
apron. You'd help her make
chicken noodle soup with
lots of yummy vegetables.
"Mmm, delicious!"

If Grandma were here,

she'd help you lace up your
roller skates. Off you go . . .
Watch out now!

If Grandma were here,

she would pick you up after you fell.

She'd put a Band-Aid on your boo-boo.

With a kiss, she'd make it all better.

If Grandma were here,

she would stretch her arms out
wide to show how much she
loves you.

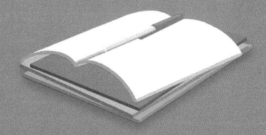

If Grandma were here,

you'd hop up on her lap. She
would read you your favorite
book. She would sing a lullaby
as you fall asleep in her arms.

Grandma is always here,

inside you, right here

in your heart.

From Dusk through Dawn

As the moon tucks in the sun and night falls,
look up to the stars. You'll hear my call.
Through your window, through sleepy trees,
past the Big Dipper and Hercules.
Breathe in deep and exhale slow.
Keep your focus, and I will show.
The twinkle in the stars, that's my hello.
It's your love that keeps me aglow.
Give a wave and blow a kiss.
Tell me all the things I've missed.
From school performances to graduation ceremonies.
Say to yourself, "Someone up there really loves me."
As time passes and life goes on,
I will always be here...from dusk through dawn.

Love,
Grandma

CPSIA information can be obtained
at www.ICGtesting.com
Printed in the USA
JSHW012155220321
12790JS00004B/22